HOW TO BE
KING OF
PRIDE ROCK

CONFIDENCE WITH SIMBA

Mari Schuh

Lerner Publications ◆ Minneapolis

For Brock, Blake, Robbie, and Dylan

Lerner Publications Company
A division of Lerner Publishing Group, Inc.
241 First Avenue North
Minneapolis, MN 55401 USA

For reading levels and more information, look up this title at www.lernerbooks.com.

Main body text set in Mikado a 14.5/22.
Typeface provided by HVD Fonts.

Library of Congress Cataloging-in-Publication Data

Names: Schuh, Mari C., 1975- author.
Title: How to be king of Pride Rock : confidence with Simba / Mari Schuh.
Other titles: Lion King (Motion picture)
Description: Minneapolis : Lerner Publications, [2019] | Series: Disney great character guides | Includes bibliographical references. | Audience: Grades K to 3.
Identifiers: LCCN 2018010739 (print) | LCCN 2018023474 (ebook) | ISBN 9781541543164 (eb pdf) | ISBN 9781541539044 (lb : alk. paper)
Subjects: LCSH: Leadership–Juvenile literature. | Lion–Juvenile literature. | Simba (Fictitious character : Disney)–Juvenile literature.
Classification: LCC BF637.L4 (ebook) | LCC BF637.L4 S355 2019 (print) | DDC 158/.4–dc23

LC record available at https://lccn.loc.gov/2018010739

Manufactured in the United States of America
1 - 45087 - 35914 - 9/6/2018

Table of Contents

The Right Candidate

So you want to rule Pride Rock and the Pride Lands, just like little Simba here will someday? Think it would be neat to be a powerful king? Well, the truth is, being a leader isn't an easy job. It takes work and a whole lot of faith in yourself. Young Simba is about to learn that!

Did You Know?

Pride Rock is where Simba and the other lions live. It's their home within the Pride Lands. The wider Pride Lands is the place the rest of the animals call home.

Being a leader of any kind is a big responsibility. This important job needs just the right candidate. It's a job for those who believe in their own abilities and care about the ones they are leading.

Simba's dad, Mufasa, has been at it a long time—he's a pro! So what does a day on the job look like for him?

A Day on the Job

King Mufasa's workday starts just as the warm sun rises. He and Simba climb way up to the top of Pride Rock. They look over the entire kingdom. It's beautiful! As king, Mufasa must trust his ability to make decisions for the good of all the animals in the Pride Lands. Every creature, big or small, is important.

"Everything you see exists together in a delicate balance," he tells Simba. "As king, you need to understand that balance and respect all the creatures. We are all connected in the great circle of life."

Did You Know?

Artists completed more than one million drawings to make *The Lion King* movie!

Someday Simba will take over as king. But until then, there's so much to learn! Today Mufasa gives Simba pouncing lessons. Simba must trust his instincts. Practice will help him learn when it is time to pounce.

Simba starts to get the hang of it—but suddenly, the bird Zazu squawks a warning. "Sire! Hyenas! In the Pride Lands!" he announces to Mufasa.

Mufasa knows he must leave to chase them away. He has confidence that he's up to the challenge. Simba wants to come too, but Mufasa orders Zazu to take him home.

Character Callout

Mufasa doesn't hesitate when a challenge arises. He has the self-assurance needed to do his job—in this case, protect the Pride Lands from hyenas.

Get the Skills

After Mufasa leaves to take care of business, Simba joins up with his best friend, Nala. Together, they go exploring. Mufasa has warned Simba never to go outside the Pride Lands. But Simba wants to visit the elephant graveyard that lies beyond his home. He wants to be confident, like his dad. But soon, the cub hears something approaching.

It's hyenas! The cubs are in danger! But just as the hyenas catch up to them, Mufasa shows up. He doesn't hesitate to do what he must to scare the beasts away. Once the danger is behind them, Mufasa and Simba have a talk.

"I was just trying to be brave, like you," Simba tells his dad.

"I'm only brave when I have to be," Mufasa replies. "Simba, being brave doesn't mean you go looking for trouble."

Character Callout

Mufasa teaches Simba a lesson about being brave. He shows that having faith in yourself is about meeting challenges when necessary— not about taking dangerous risks.

Simba thinks about that. "But you're not scared of anything," he says.

"I was today. I thought I might lose you."

Simba realizes something then: "I guess even kings get scared."

Did You Know?

A lion's roar is loud! In fact, it's the loudest among the cat family. It can be heard as far as 5 miles (8 km) away.

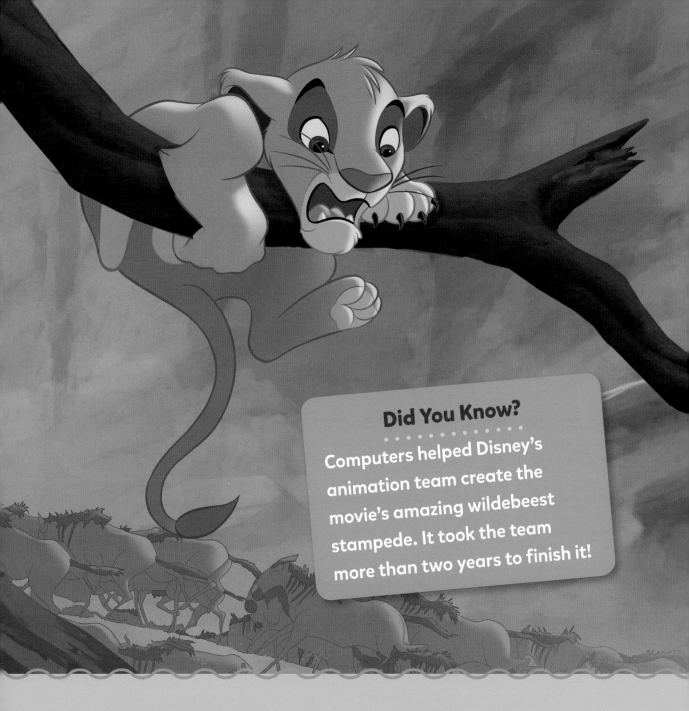

Did You Know?

Computers helped Disney's animation team create the movie's amazing wildebeest stampede. It took the team more than two years to finish it!

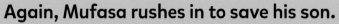

Simba escaped the hyenas once. But they are still causing trouble—and so is Simba's mean uncle, Scar. Back home in the Pride Lands, Scar tells Simba to sit on a rock and wait for a surprise. But it's a trick. The hyenas scare a herd of wildebeests. The wildebeests run toward little Simba. He's in trouble again and must climb a tree for safety.

Again, Mufasa rushes in to save his son.

Career Connection: Teachers
· · · · · · · · ·
Just like Mufasa, teachers are there to help. They provide safe environments where their students can learn, and they aren't afraid to step in when tricky questions or problems come up.

With Simba out of harm's way, Mufasa tries to climb a cliff where he knows beasts can't reach him and Simba. But the cliff is too steep. "Brother, help me!" he calls to Scar. But the evil Scar lets Mufasa fall.

Simba rushes to his dad. But it's too late. Mufasa didn't survive when Scar let him drop. Simba thinks it's his fault. He questions his own worth and runs far, far away.

Growing and Learning

✦ ✦ ✦

Simba runs until he collapses from exhaustion. When he wakes up from a deep sleep, a warthog and a meerkat greet him. Simba still feels sad, but Pumbaa the warthog and Timon the meerkat tell him things don't have to be so glum. They explain to Simba that they don't believe in worrying.

Simba considers that. He starts to understand what his new friends are saying. He decides to stay with them in the jungle and put his past behind him.

Time passes, and Simba grows into an adult. Meanwhile, even in their carefree lives, Pumbaa and Timon do run into trouble. One day, a hungry lioness chases Pumbaa. Simba steps up to fight the lioness. But then he realizes something: the lioness is Nala! The two happily reunite.

But Nala tells Simba terrible news about the Pride Lands. With Simba and Mufasa gone, Scar has taken over as king. He's let the hyenas invade. They've ruined the land. The Pride Lands have no food or water. Nala reminds Simba he has responsibilities back home.

Career Connection: Environmental Engineer

Like the animals of the Pride Lands, human communities sometimes face challenges with land and water. Environmental engineers work to solve these problems. They find ways to keep land and water safe for the people and animals that live there.

But Simba's still feeling sad about his dad. He isn't sure he can fulfill his responsibilities. He doesn't think he's cut out to lead the Pride Lands.

Got the Dream Job!

That night, Simba sees the spirit of the great, wise Mufasa. Mufasa's spirit tells Simba that he *is* the king.

Simba reflects on those words and starts to believe in himself. He decides his dad is right. He is worthy, and he is king. He has to save the Pride Lands from Scar!

Character Callout

· · · · · · · · · · · · · · ·

Simba decides to face his past. He shows resilience, or the ability to bounce back from hard times, by deciding to return to the Pride Lands. He takes on the challenge even though he'd been doubting himself.

Simba returns to the Pride Lands, and his friends join him. Simba is grateful for their help and support. Timon and Pumbaa let the hyenas chase them so Simba and Nala can sneak by.

Simba wastes no time in approaching his uncle. And now that he's in power, Scar is truly letting his evil nature show. He even hisses in Simba's ear that he was the one who killed Mufasa!

Career Connection: Mayor

· · · · · ·

A mayor is the leader of a city. Mayors must trust their own judgment, but they also need the help of the city council and city workers. Together, they all make the city a good place to live.

Simba pins Scar to the ground. He makes him tell the other animals the truth about Mufasa. When they find out Scar killed their leader, they all join in to take down the evil lion and the hyenas. Simba and his friends save the Pride Lands!

Simba officially has a new job. He's king. Simba has courage, confidence, and a sense of responsibility. With the support of his family and friends, he knows he's ready to lead. Today is a great day for the Pride Lands!

All in a Day's Work

As king, Simba needs to have faith in his own abilities.
Which of your abilities are you proud of?
Are you a good singer? A fantastic soccer player? A wonderful
friend? We all have skills we can feel good about.

When have you felt the most confident?

How can you remind others that they
have value?

"This is my home."

Glossary

candidate: someone who is seeking a job

confidence: a feeling of trust or belief

instinct: a natural ability

kingdom: a country or area that is ruled by a king or queen

resilience: the ability to become strong, healthy, or successful again after something bad happens

responsibility: a duty or a job. Someone who is responsible follows rules and keeps promises.

worth: value or importance

To Learn More

Books
Bell, Samantha S. *Meet a Baby Lion.* Minneapolis: Lerner Publications, 2016.
Learn how baby lions, just like young Simba, grow and change to become strong adult lions.

Schuh, Mari. *How to Be a Snow Queen: Leadership with Elsa.* Minneapolis: Lerner Publications, 2019.
Come along with Elsa and learn about another great character trait to have—leadership!

Websites
Disney: *The Lion King*
https://movies.disney.com/the-lion-king
Have more fun with *Lion King* activities. Learn how to draw Timon, make a *Lion King* mask, and enjoy mazes, games, and coloring pages.

Oh My Disney: Life Lessons from *The Lion King*
https://ohmy.disney.com/movies/2015/04/18/life-lessons-from-the-lion-king/
Visit this website to learn ten important life lessons from *The Lion King.*